A LOAD
of DANGER

Margaret Scariano

A **HIGH ADVENTURE** BOOK
High Noon Books
Novato, California

Cover Design: Jim McConnell
Interior Illustrations: Herb Heidinger

International Standard Book Number: 0-87879-406-9

9 8 7 6 5 4 3 2 1 0
7 6 5 4 3 2 1 0 9 8

High Noon Books
a division of ATP
20 Commercial Blvd.
Novato, California 94949

Contents

Chapter 1

Great News!

Dan was the next one in line. He held his breath. He tried to hear what the foreman was saying to the guy ahead of him. He had to get hired. He had been out of a job for three months. He didn't even know what he would do next. He needed this job.

He heard the foreman ask the man, "What kind of experience do you have?"

Experience? The foreman wanted to know what kinds of jobs the man had held. Dan's hopes sank. The guy was writing down all his truck driving jobs. And what a list! What chance did Dan have now? He felt foolish. Maybe he shouldn't even wait.

The foreman said, "Thanks for coming by. We'll let you know." The man walked off. Dan watched the foreman write something on a piece of paper. Then he looked up and said, "Next."

Dan stepped up to the table where the foreman sat.

"Name?" The foreman didn't even look up.

"Dan Reardon, sir."

"Experience?"

"None that I was paid for. But I have driven trucks. All kinds. And I have a good driving record."

The foreman looked up. "You do, huh?" He grinned. "Well, son, we might just have to give you some experience. Paying experience, that is."

Had he heard right? Was this man really going to hire him? Dan waited at the table. He was afraid to speak. Maybe he would say something wrong—something that would keep him from getting the job.

"Okay, Dan. Fill out this application. Turn it into the office. You're hired. You'll be a part-time driver. Welcome to the Brook Garbage Company." The foreman stood up. He shook hands with Dan. Then he said to the other men in line, "The driving job has been filled, men. Thanks for coming by."

Dan sat at the table and filled out the application form. He took it to the office. The foreman was waiting outside.

"Dan, I'd like you to meet a couple of guys.

They work part-time, too. Will Sands and Billy Harris." The men shook hands.

"Is Dan going to work Mondays and Tuesdays?" Will asked.

"Yes. You and Billy will take turns the other four days."

"Any chance of full-time work coming up, Mr. Johnson?" Billy asked.

"Not right now. But we'll hire full-time men later from our part-time help," Mr. Johnson said.

"Thanks for the job, Mr. Johnson. I'll be here at 6:00 tomorrow morning."

Dan could hardly wait to get home. His mother would be happy. Dad had died a year ago. Since then it had been hard for Mom and him. Part-time work wouldn't solve all their money problems. But with his mother's sewing business plus his salary they'd make it. Maybe he could get another part-time job for the rest of the week.

Dan drove home. He felt great. He had a job!

At home he could hear his mother busy at the sewing machine. Dan wanted to be "cool" about his new job. But he was so excited, he shouted from the kitchen, "Mom! Mom! Guess what?"

"I can't hear you, Dan. Come in the sewing

room."

He hurried down the hall to the sewing room. "Stop that machine, Mom. I've got great news."

With a sigh she stopped and turned around. "Honestly, Dan, you're like a little kid sometimes. You know I can't hear with this sewing machine going." She reached for his hand. "Sit. Now what's the big news?" She smiled at him.

"I've got a job! I start tomorrow morning." Then Dan told her all about the job.

"Well, son, this calls for a celebration. It's chocolate cake with chocolate frosting for dessert!"

That night Dan planned how he'd work hard and soon be put on full-time. Then maybe his mother wouldn't have to work so hard. The next morning he was up early and he was nervous. He just had to do a good job!

The next two weeks Dan drove the truck on Monday and Tuesday. He drove carefully. He was cheerful with the customers. He was even beginning to know some of them. And he didn't waste time. This job was important to him.

On the third Monday morning Mr. Johnson was waiting for him. Dan parked his car in the employees' lot. He walked toward the garbage truck. What did Mr. Johnson want? He looked at his watch. He wasn't late. Did someone complain about his work? He didn't think so. He hadn't had any trouble with the truck either. He took a deep breath.

"Good morning, Mr. Johnson."

"Glad you're a few minutes early, Dan. I want to talk with you."

"Sure. I hope nothing's wrong." Dan tried to sound as if everything were OK. Inside he felt shakey. Like something was up. But he didn't know what it could be.

Chapter 2

The Good and the Bad

Mr. Johnson stared at him. At first he didn't say anything. It seemed forever before he spoke. "Well, Dan, I've been watching you these last few weeks. You're a good worker."

Dan felt a lot better. "Thanks, Mr. Johnson. I give my best," he said.

"I know you do. That's why I am going to put your name at the top of the part-time drivers' list."

"That's great. But what does that mean?" Dan asked.

"It means that you fill in for a regular driver. Say a full-time driver calls in sick. I call you first to take his place." Mr. Johnson smiled.

"Because my name is on the top?" Dan asked.

"Right. It'll give you a chance to earn some extra money. Also, you'll get more experience."

Then Dan thought of Will Sands and Billy

Harris. Both of them had been at Brook Garbage Company longer than he. Was it fair for his name to move to the top? He thought about the extra money. It would really help. And with more experience he would have a better chance at a full-time driving job. A guy had to look after himself, didn't he? Still, it wouldn't hurt to ask.

"What about Will and Billy, Mr. Johnson? 1 really want the extra work. But they've been here longer," Dan said.

"Listen, Dan. I run this company on good service — not how long anyone has worked here. Got it?"

"Yes, sir. Got it." Dan opened the door to the truck and got in. "Thanks, Mr. Johnson."

Mr. Johnson waved to Dan. "You're all right, kid."

Dan backed the truck out of the lot. He still wasn't sure about Billy and Will. But he felt good about himself. At last good things were happening.

He drove along streets lined with trees. Customers smiled at him. One lady called from her porch, "Wait, young man. I've got something for you." She ran out with a doughnut and a paper cup filled with coffee. "You were so nice last week. You cleaned up the curb after those kids knocked over my garbage can. This is to thank you."

"Tastes great. Thanks," Dan called as he drove away.

On the next street three garbage cans in a row had been dumped over. Still Dan felt good. He whistled while he shoveled the trash into the truck.

A young boy on a bike pulled up next to Dan. He was wearing a baseball uniform.

"Hey, mister. Want to buy a ticket?" he asked Dan.

"Ticket for what?" Dan smiled to himself. The boy's baseball cap was too big. It came down almost to his eyes.

"Our game on Sunday. We're playing the Eagles. And my team's going to win."

"Sure, I'll buy a couple. Where do you play?"

"Lake Powell Park. The game starts at 5:30 sharp. Well, sometimes we're a little late." The boy tore two tickets from a booklet. "And I'm the pitcher."

Dan paid the boy. It might be fun to watch the young kids play ball. "See you at the game," Dan called. He climbed into his truck.

All morning long Dan drove up one street and down another. He must have loaded a hundred cans of garbage.

But he wasn't thinking about the number of cans. He was thinking about his future. Already he was top man on the part-time drivers' list. Maybe soon he'd get on full-time. And one day maybe he'd own his own trucking company.

It was just one o'clock. Dan drove into the

"Hey, Mister, want to buy a ticket?"

Brook Garbage Company parking lot. His route was finished for the day. He still had to wash the truck. But then he could go home.

He parked the truck near the hose. He unrolled the hose and began squirting water on the hood. He didn't see Will and Billy. They came from behind the truck.

"What do you think you're doing, Reardon?" Billy asked. His face was red. He looked angry.

"Taking care of the truck, Billy." Dan sprayed the windshield.

"Taking care of yourself is more like it." Will stood beside Billy.

Dan shut the water off. He turned and faced the men. "What do you mean?"

"You know. Playing up to the boss. Cutting us out," Billy said.

"Yeah. Me and Billy have been here longer. It's not right that you're ahead of us on the part-time drivers' list."

"Listen, guys, I had nothing to do with my name going to the top of the list. Believe me."

"Believe you? After what you did? Not on your life." Will glared at Dan.

"You cut us out, Reardon. And we don't take that lying down." Billy turned on his heel and walked off. Will followed him.

"Hey, guys, ask Mr. Johnson then. He'll tell you. I never did anything to get to the top of the list. Just ask him," Dan called after them. But the two men kept walking.

He finished cleaning the truck. But now he was worried. He didn't want Will and Billy angry. It really wasn't his fault that Mr. Johnson put him first. Finally he decided there wasn't anything he could do to make them feel better. He hoped they'd get over being mad.

But two days later Dan knew that they—or someone else—was very angry with him.

Chapter 3

Dented Hopes

Dan couldn't believe that anyone would try to hurt him. But two days after Will and Billy had yelled at him, it happened.

The telephone rang at five-thirty Thursday morning. Dan had rushed into the kitchen to answer. He didn't want the ring to wake his mother. He grabbed the receiver.

"Hello," he said softly.

"Hello, Reardon. This is Mr. Johnson, the foreman at the Brook Garbage Company. Our regular driver called in sick a few minutes ago. I need you to drive his truck."

"Sure, Mr. Johnson." Dan was wide awake now. A full day's work!

"Fine. Get down here right away, OK?"

"Yes, sir."

"And, Reardon, get moving, will you? You have to get out of the lot by six. Otherwise, you

12

won't finish the route on time."

Dan dressed quickly. He didn't even take time for a cup of coffee. At the Brook Garbage Company parking lot Mr. Johnson stood by the truck. Dan parked his car and hurried over.

Mr. Johnson looked at his watch. "You made good time. Here—look at this map. This is the route you'll take."

Dan studied the map. The route was well laid out. He knew he'd have no trouble following it. "I understand this map, Mr. Johnson. No problem." He folded the map and opened the door to the truck. He laid the map on the passenger's seat. "It's almost six. I better get going."

"Right. I'll see you back here at four," Mr. Johnson said.

Dan started the engine. He rolled the window down and called out, "Thanks for the job today, Mr. Johnson."

The foreman waved.

Dan backed the truck up. He turned his wheels and shifted into first gear. There was no traffic. He pulled onto the main road.

The morning air was clear. The sky was blue. Dan felt good. A full day's work! He was glad that neither Billy nor Will had showed up. They still weren't talking to him. And he didn't want anything to spoil this great day.

He headed for his first garbage pick-up. It was just over the hill. He shifted into second. At the top of the hill Dan looked down to the drive-in theater. That was his first stop.

The truck rolled over the top of the hill. Dan shifted into third and started down the steep hill. The truck picked up speed. Dan pressed on the brake pedal. His foot went to the floor board. No brakes! Faster and faster the truck rolled down the hill. Dan tried to shift down. But the truck was going too fast. At least there was no traffic. Maybe he could steer the truck until it rolled to a stop. Sweat poured off his forehead. His hands felt slippery on the wheel. He rolled his window down. There was just one curve. If only he could make that turn! And if another car heading his way wasn't making the same turn. He spun the wheel wide. He planned to cut to the left after the turn. The tires squealed as he banked the curve. The smell of hot rubber filled the truck cab. Then he saw disaster. A small pick-up truck was entering the highway. Dan had two choices. He could smash into the pick-up. Or he could take the ditch. He turned sharply to the right. The truck missed the small pick-up. It bumped over the ruts in the narrow ditch. The truck tipped to the right — then to the left. Was it going to roll over? Dan gripped the wheel tightly. Was the truck ever going to stop? Then Dan was spinning over and over in the truck cab.

A few seconds later he heard a voice. "Are you all right in there?"

"I think so." Dan moved his arms and legs.

"Give me your hand," the voice said. "I'll help you out the window."

Dan stuck out his hand. Someone pulled him through the window. Dan saw the small pick-up parked on the side of the road.

"Sure glad you missed me," the driver of the pick-up said. "You all right?"

"Yeah. But my truck."

"There doesn't seem to be much damage. Just a few dents here and there," the driver said. "I bet if we got it off its side, it would run fine."

"You think so?" Dan started to feel better. He'd have to report the accident to Mr. Johnson. But if he could finish his route, it wouldn't seem so bad.

"Sure. I've got four-wheel drive on my pick-up. Lots of traction. We'll just hook a chain on your truck frame. It will just take a minute."

The driver was right. In a short time Dan was ready to drive the garbage truck onto the highway. The pick-up driver wrote his name on a piece of paper. "You give this to your boss. Tell him I'll be calling him. I want him to know how you kept from hitting me. I should have looked both ways. I could have been killed." He shook Dan's hand and walked to his pick-up.

Dan slowly drove to a telephone booth. He parked in a large lot. He needed plenty of room to stop the truck. He called Mr. Johnson. He told him he wasn't hurt and the truck drove fine. "It doesn't have any brakes though. But it does have some new dents, Mr. Johnson."

"Glad you weren't hurt, Dan. I can't figure out why the brakes went out. I know for a fact that truck was just checked. We've got good mechanics, too." Then Mr. Johnson asked, "Think you feel like finishing the route?"

"Sure. I'm fine."

"I'll get another truck out to you right away. Go get a cup of coffee or something while you're waiting."

"All right. I'll see you at four."

Dan had just finished his second cup of coffee when the other truck drove up. He watched as his dented truck turned to the Brook Garbage Company. Then he started on his route again in the new truck.

The rest of the day passed with no trouble. In his mind Dan went over the accident again and again. There was no way he could have stopped it. But who had fooled with his brakes? And why?

It couldn't have been Mr. Johnson, Dan thought. He had no reason. The mechanics? Why? They were proud of their work. Then he had another thought. Billy and Will. Would they go that far? Would they knock out the brakes to get him out of the way?

Chapter 4

Another Chance

Dan washed the truck. He was glad no one was around. He hated to face the foreman. Here Mr. Johnson had given him a chance. And what did he do? Pile up the truck. He hoped he wasn't blamed for the accident. He had to keep this job. He rolled up the hose again. The truck was clean for tomorrow's route. Mr. Johnson came out of the office. "How do you feel, Dan?"

"Fine, Mr. Johnson. I didn't get hurt. Have the mechanics found out why the brakes didn't work?"

Dan saw Mr. Johnson frown. He said, "Yeah, they found out, all right. Some joker drained the brake fluid out."

Dan's heart seemed to stop. A chill ran down his back. "It must have been a mistake. No one would do that on purpose."

Mr. Johnson stared at him for a moment.

"You have no idea who might drain the fluid?" he asked.

Dan didn't look at Mr. Johnson. It could have been Will or Billy. But he had no proof. He looked at Mr. Johnson and shook his head. "No, I have no idea who'd fool with the brakes."

Mr. Johnson nodded. "All right, Dan. But if you hear anything, let me know." He patted him on the back. "Go on home. Glad you weren't hurt."

Dan walked to his car in the parking lot. It'd been quite a day. When he got to his car, Billy was leaning against the fender. "Hey, Reardon, heard you had some trouble today."

"Yes, someone drained the brake fluid."

"You don't say. Must have been a joke," Billy said.

Dan opened the car door. He slid behind the wheel. "Mr. Johnson didn't seem to think it was too funny."

Billy walked up to the car window. He leaned down and looked straight at Dan. "It might be worse next time. Think about that." Then he turned and walked away.

All the way home that's all Dan thought about. Should he tell Mr. Johnson what Billy had said? He didn't want to cause trouble. He just wanted to work.

He pulled into his driveway. He knew one thing for sure. Before he took the next truck out, he was going to check the brakes!

That evening Dan turned on television. He didn't care what was on. Anything. Just so he didn't have to think about today's accident. But even a comedy show couldn't block out his thoughts. He changed the channel. Maybe another program would help. He slumped down in front of the set again.

"Goodness, Dan, you're restless tonight. That's the third time you've changed programs. Is something bothering you?" his mother asked.

Dan didn't answer right away. He didn't want to lie. But he didn't want to worry his mother about his job either. He answered, "Guess I'm still thinking about the job." He picked up the newspaper and turned to the want ads. Maybe he'd just find other work. He didn't need the kind of hassle he'd had today. He checked each ad. Nothing he could do. He'd just have to see this job through and hope for the best.

On Monday Dan reported for his regular shift. He checked to be sure the brakes worked. He was ready to leave. Mr. Johnson yelled at him, "Hey, wait. I need to talk with you."

Dan shut off the engine and climbed out of the truck. Out of the corner of his eyes he saw Will watching him. Billy stopped changing a tire and stared. Dan felt a shiver of fear. What were they planning to do next?

Mr. Johnson put his arm around Dan's shoulder. He moved him away from Billy and Will. "Dan, when you finish your route, stop by this address. Give the man this envelope. It's a price list."

"The man will give you something to bring back to me." Mr. Johnson looked at the ground. He seemed nervous. "Be careful with the package. It's valuable." He looked at Dan. He added, "Contracts and stuff like that. You know."

"I'll take good care of it. I'd better get going. I'll be late." Dan jogged toward his truck. He wondered why Mr. Johnson seemed so nervous.

"Dan! Oh, Dan!" Mr. Johnson called.

Dan stopped and turned.

"Don't give that package to anyone but me. Got that?"

"Just you. Right."

"Yeah. It's sort of a surprise for the big boss."

"Right." Dan headed for his truck.

The route went well. And the truck was working

"The man will give you something to bring back to me. Be careful with the package."

great. I should feel happy, Dan thought. No problems with the customers. No problems with the truck. But I don't feel quite right. Like something's going to go wrong.

He emptied the last garbage can into the truck. He climbed into the cab. His route was finished. He looked at the address on the envelope. He knew where it was—in the factory part of the city.

He shifted into first and made a right turn. After all, Mr. Johnson was the foreman. And he, Dan Reardon, wasn't paid to have feelings. Either good ones or bad ones!

He drove into the Miner Labs parking lot. He hoped he wouldn't see anyone he knew. Dad used to work at Miner Labs. A man stood by the doorway to the office. "Got something for me?" he asked.

Dan handed him the envelope. The man tore it open and quickly read it. Then he reached inside his coat pocket. He took out a thick envelope. He handed it to Dan. It had Mr. Johnson's name on it. The man said, "Tell Johnson, the sooner the better." He turned and walked back into the office.

Chapter 5

Moonlighting

Dan put the thick envelope on the seat. He headed for the Brook Garbage Company. Something bothered him. That envelope. It sure didn't feel like contracts and stuff like that.

Waiting for the light to change, he touched the envelope. It felt like money. Lots of money. He held the envelope up to the light. It had a green glow.

Someone honked behind him. He shifted gears and drove on. His thoughts were still on the envelope. Why was he worrying about it? It wasn't his job to guess — or to judge. His job was to do a good job. And to keep his job.

Mr. Johnson must have been waiting for him. Dan had barely pulled into the parking lot when Mr. Johnson came running out of the office. He hurried to Dan.

"Did you handle that matter for me,

Reardon?" Mr. Johnson asked.

"Yes, sir." Dan walked to the hose hanging on a hook.

"Well, did you bring back anything for me?" Mr. Johnson's voice sounded harsh.

"It's on the seat," Dan said. For some reason he didn't want to hand the envelope to Mr. Johnson. Like it was dirty or something.

The foreman ran around to the passenger side of the truck. He yanked open the door. Dan watched him open the envelop. Mr. Johnson smiled as he put the envelope in his inside jacket pocket.

"Thanks, Reardon. See you later." Mr. Johnson walked quickly back to the office. He was whistling. Almost like there was music in the envelope, Dan thought.

The next day Dan did his job with no special orders from Mr. Johnson. He cleaned up his truck after the route. The worries he'd felt yesterday seemed sort of stupid today. He should have used his common sense. So what if there was money in the envelope? There must be a reason for it. One thing he knew for sure. He had a job. And he had to keep it.

He had a surprise planned for his mother. With his part-time work and just one or two extra day's work he could save money. Then at the end of the summer they could go to the beach for a weekend.

He remembered the beach house they'd rented two years ago. He and Dad had fished in the surf. He and his mother had collected shells on the sandy beach. They'd explored the tide pools in the morning. They swam in the ocean in the afternoon. Dan still remembered the surprised look on his mother's face. A wave had caught her. It lifted her to its crest. Then it dropped her in the foamy water. She'd washed to shore like a piece of driftwood.

At night they built a huge beach fire. Other people along the beach joined them. They sang songs. They roasted marshmallows. The last night they had a fish fry. Dan still remembered how good the crisp, fresh fish tasted.

That last night the fog had rolled in. It shut out the beach cabins, the city lights, and the ships' lights at sea. Dan had felt as if the campers had their own private room in the world. He could hardly wait to surprise his mother with another trip to the beach.

He hung the hose back on its rack. Whistling, he headed for his car.

Later that week Mr. Johnson called him at home. "Hey, there, Dan. Johnson here. I was wondering if you'd like to make some extra money. Do a little extra work."

"You bet." Dan's hopes for a weekend at the beach grew higher. "When do you need me, Mr. Johnson?"

"You remember where you delivered the contracts for me? You know—Miner Labs."

"Sure. I remember."

"Well, this is a special job for them. Come to the Brook Garbage Company at 11:00 tonight. I'll be waiting."

A few minutes before 11:00 Dan drove into the Brook Garbage Company lot. There was a truck parked close to the exit. But nobody was around. It was kind of spooky. Just him and a truck in an empty lot. Well, at least, he didn't have to put up with Will and Billy. Then he began to worry. Was this the wrong night?

He climbed out of his car and headed for the parked truck. It wasn't a garbage truck, but more like a big van. In the dim light he couldn't read the company's name on the truck's side. He was a few feet from the front bumper. A man stepped out of the shadows.

"Dan, is that you?"

It was Mr. Johnson's voice. There was no need to be nervous. But Dan's heart beat faster anyway. "I'm ready, Mr. Johnson."

"The truck's loaded. Ready for take-off." Mr. Johnson handed him a map. "Look this over real good, Reardon. I think it's clear enough. If you have any questions, I'll be here for another five minutes."

Dan turned on the cab light. He spread the map over the steering wheel. The route didn't seem too hard. He knew all the main streets on the map. He rolled down his window. "I'm ready, Mr. Johnson."

"Fine. You shouldn't have any trouble. I'll be waiting for you," Mr. Johnson said.

"You just want me to dump the stuff that's in the van and come back? Right?"

"That's right."

Dan nodded. He rolled up the window. He started the engine. He was on his way. What an easy way to make a buck or two!

The stars were out. The moon really did look like a huge piece of cheese. A perfect night for extra work. Dan smiled to himself.

There was very little traffic. Soon Dan was turning off the main highway onto a dirt road. He stopped the truck. Turning on the light, he looked at the map again. Three miles farther. He turned off the inside light. It sure was dark. No street lights, no headlights from traffic, no homes lit up. He folded the map again and drove down the road.

Three miles down the road he reached the spot on the map. He thought he knew this area. He wasn't far from Lake Powell Park. It was just over the hill from here. Now he knew exactly where he was. At the city's empty garbage dump. The city had closed it three or four years ago. It was strange to be dumping something here. He got out of the truck. Using his flashlight, he walked to the back of the truck. He opened the door. He flashed his light around to see what had to be dumped. There were large barrels. They filled the back of the van. He looked closer at the printing on one of the barrels. Oh, no! Dan stepped back from the truck.

Chapter 6

Dark Decisions

And now he knew. He had been right to be worried. This was real trouble. Real danger. And worst of all—now it was his problem. What was he going to do?

The barrels were filled with wastes from the nuclear lab. That was the reason for dumping the barrels at night. That was the reason for the money in the envelope. And that was the reason why he, Dan Reardon, had been chosen for the job. Because he didn't have experience. Because he was eager to please. Because he needed the job so badly.

What a bozo he was! He wondered if Johnson had asked Will or Billy first. Probably. They were experienced drivers. But they had turned him down. They weren't about to drive around in the middle of the night with wastes from the nuclear lab. They'd worked long enough for the company that they felt safe in their jobs. They didn't jump every time Johnson looked at them. Sweat broke out on Dan's forehead. He felt taken advantage of. Because he was inexperienced, he'd been set up.

Now he was angry. Needing the job so badly, he'd been the perfect man for Johnson. Dan remembered how hard he'd tried to be polite, to do the best job possible. What a fool he'd been. He started back to the cab of the truck. Just because he didn't have much experience was no reason to continue to be a willing victim.

But maybe he was wrong. Surely, the lab or Mr. Johnson wouldn't get rid of unsafe nuclear wastes this way. They knew what they were doing. Maybe they just wanted to dump the barrels at night so people wouldn't worry. Dan almost laughed aloud. Yeah, that was it. It had to be that.

He set the flashlight on the bed of the truck. He climbed inside. Might as well get the job done and get home, he thought. He pulled one barrel closer to the tail-gate. Then he shoved another one closer. He grabbed the third one. The barrel felt damp. He reached for his flashlight and shone it on the barrel. It was leaking! He jumped back as if he had touched a snake. And, in a way, it was almost the same thing. The waste in this barrel was as deadly as any snake's poison. What should he do? Find a phone and call Mr. Johnson? No, that wouldn't work. Mr. Johnson wouldn't answer a phone at this hour. But he had to do something. A leaky barrel could poison the whole area. And him, too! Quickly he jumped out of the truck.

He could hear a dog barking. There must be homes not too far from here, Dan thought. Homes that would be in danger from what was in those barrels.

Then he thought of Lake Powell Park. It was just over the hill. Close enough so that families and kids were in danger.

With flashlight in hand Dan walked a little ways from the truck. He saw signs: "No Dumping," "Dump Closed," "Keep Out, Private Property."

How could he just dump those barrels and drive away? But if he didn't follow Johnson's orders, he'd have no job. No extra money for a weekend at the beach. Maybe he should just do the job. After all, he would just be following orders. He wouldn't be to blame.

But he was a member of the human race. Wasn't it his duty to protect his fellow man?

The waste in the barrel was deadly as any snake poison.

What if, later, he heard that someone had got sick?

Dan couldn't make up his mind. First he thought one way—then another. Now the night air had turned cool. He shivered and stuck his hands in his pocket. He felt something. The tickets for the kids' ball game. He'd forgotten to go. He smiled to himself as he thought of the little boy. Wonder if he won his game. Dan remembered the baseball hat the boy wore. It was much too big for him. He was a good kid. He pitched. He sold tickets. He was loyal to his team. What more could he do?

Dan turned and walked to the truck. Now he knew what he had to do.

Chapter 7

Surprise Visitor

Dan climbed in the truck bed. He shoved the barrels back in place. Then he jumped down and closed the door.

All sorts of questions worried him. Had he been poisoned? What could he do to protect himself? Should he report this to the police? He got in the truck. He backed away from the dumping hole. He turned the truck around and headed back to the Brook Garbage Company.

His stomach felt funny—like he'd eaten too much—or not enough. The steering wheel was slick in his sweaty hands. Again and again he asked himself, how could Mr. Johnson do this to me—and to the other people in the town? He was at the main road now.

He pulled onto the highway. Again his thoughts returned to Mr. Johnson. Maybe the foreman didn't know what was in the barrels.

Maybe he'll be as surprised as I was. Yeah, maybe, you yahoo, Dan told himself. Maybe Johnson sized you up right. A guy who needed to work. Eager to please. Hungry for money. A real dummy! He had a bitter taste in his mouth. Suddenly he felt very tired.

He was on the edge of the city now. Ahead he saw the lights of a twenty-four-hour gas station. He decided to stop and scrub his hands — just to be on the safe side. After washing up, he climbed back in the truck. He didn't know whether the scrubbing helped. But it made him feel better.

He started to pull onto the highway. In the dark he hadn't seen the deep pot-hole in the road. The right front tire hit the hole with a jolt. Dan heard a noise in the back end. He steered the truck carefully so that the rear wheel wouldn't hit the hole. Now he had a new worry. Would the barrels explode? Could a jolt set them off? He slowed the truck down. He didn't want any sudden stops or bumps.

His hands felt itchy. Was that how radiation burns felt? And his throat. It was dry and scratchy. Would this nightmare ever end?

He slowed down his speed even more. It seemed to be taking forever to get back to the Brook Garbage Company. He thought of Mr.

Johnson. Dan wanted to talk with that guy—and fast. First of all, it was not legal to dump radioactive wastes just anywhere. And Mr. Johnson hadn't been honest with him. He had tried to make Dan a part of an unlawful act. To make it worse, the foreman had showed no interest in Dan or the people in the town. All he wanted was the money. Boy! He's lucky I'm not a fighting guy. I'd punch his lights out. But good. And lose my job, Dan thought. But after I tell him what I think, I'll lose my job anyway. But at least I can face myself in the mirror again.

He turned off the highway into the Brook Garbage Company driveway. There were lights on in the office. Guess Johnson is waiting to return the truck, Dan thought.

He parked near the office and got out and walked slowly toward it. He sure hated to give up this job. But he knew he was right. He didn't want to be mixed up in any funny business.

He opened the office door and walked down the hall to Johnson's office. He heard voices. Johnson had someone in his office with him. Dan didn't want to tell about the leaking barrels in front of someone else. But such news couldn't wait until morning. Maybe he could ask Mr. Johnson to step out in the hall for a minute. Yes, that's what he'd do.

He knocked on Mr. Johnson's office door and walked in. Billy Harris was there with Mr. Johnson. Was he doing extra work, too? Then Dan looked at Mr. Johnson. He was handcuffed.

Then Dan looked at Mr. Johnson. He was handcuffed.

Chapter 8

A Good Man

Now what? Was Billy Harris robbing Mr. Johnson? Dan was angry with Mr. Johnson. But he sure didn't want to see him robbed. Dan just stood there. He didn't know what to do next.

"Well, well. If it isn't the night driver. Sit right over there, Dan Reardon." Billy Harris pointed to a chair in front of the desk.

It was easy to obey. Billy held a pistol.

"Don't say anything, kid. He can't prove anything," Mr. Johnson said.

"Prove? He's already proved something. He's got the gun." Dan wished he could disappear. All this was like a bad dream. Here he had come back ready to tell Mr. Johnson what he thought of him. And now he was feeling sorry for him because Mr. Johnson was being held up.

Billy Harris picked up the telephone. He dialed a number.

"What's going on?" Dan asked.

"Just keep quiet, kid. I'll get to you later." Then he spoke into the telephone. "Chief, this is Harris. I've got them. Yes, with the goods. I'm sure the evidence will stand up in court. Yes, sir. I'll read them their rights. Send the police van to the Brook Garbage Company. Thanks." He hung up the telephone.

Dan sat quietly for a moment. This wasn't a robbery. It was an arrest! "Billy, what's going on? Am I under arrest or something?"

"Don't play innocent, kid. I've been keeping my eye on you. I saw you with Johnson. You delivered a special package for him and came back with an envelope. It was fat with money, I'm sure. A pay-off. And you're part of it."

"You've got to be kidding. Who are you anyway?" Dan asked.

"I work for the government. And the government doesn't allow unlawful dumping of toxic wastes. I've been working undercover for more than six months. But it's paid off. We knew the Miner Lab was getting rid of their wastes. And we were sure they were breaking the law. But we didn't know how. Then we got a tip on strange trucks entering and leaving the Brooks Garbage Company lot. That's when I went undercover."

Dan sighed. "Boy! Am I glad to know that. I thought you were a robber." He laughed.

"Shut up, Dan. He's bluffing. He's got no real evidence. Not if you keep your mouth shut," Mr. Johnson said.

"But I've got nothing to hide." Dan looked at Billy Harris.

Billy stood with his arms folded across his chest. He raised his eyebrows, but said nothing.

Dan went on talking. "You're right, Billy. I was the one who took a package to Miner Labs. Mr. Johnson said there were contracts and stuff in it. And I brought back a thick envelope and gave it to Mr. Johnson."

"So, Dan, then you are guilty, too," Billy said.

"No, I'm not. I didn't know what was in the package or the envelope. I was just following orders." Dan was beginning to get scared. What if the police didn't believe him? What if they arrested him. He thought about his mother. What would she do?

"Listen, Dan. For your own good I don't think you should do any more talking. Get a lawyer. Let him talk for you," Billy said. Billy looked more sad than angry.

Dan was quiet a moment. Then he started getting mad. He wasn't guilty of anything but following orders. No one was going to make him feel that way. "Listen, Billy, I don't need a lawyer. I didn't do anything wrong."

"All right. Maybe you were just following orders. But tonight you were the driver. And you knew what was in those barrels. And you must have known it's wrong to dump toxic wastes in a town garbage dump. So, wise up, Dan. Get a lawyer. A smart one. You'll need one to get you off."

Dan slapped his hand on the desk. "Will you stop talking and listen for a minute? That's what I'm trying to tell you, Billy. I didn't dump the barrels."

Mr. Johnson groaned, "Now you've done it."

Billy's mouth dropped open. "You didn't? What did you do with them?"

"Well, when I saw what was in them, I knew it was dangerous to leave them at the town dump. You know, Lake Powell Park is just over the hill from that old dump."

Billy walked over to Dan. "What did you do with them?" he asked.

"I brought them back here." Dan turned and looked at Mr. Johnson. "I just couldn't do it. The whole town might have been in danger."

Billy laughed out loud. "You brought them

back? Dan, oh Dan, you're my kind of man!" Then he stopped smiling. "And you knew you would lose your job — that must have been tough, Dan."

Dan looked Billy straight in the eye. "No, Billy. It was easy. My Dad worked at Miner Labs. He died last year with cancer."

"No, Billy, it was easy. My dad worked at Minor Labs. He died last year with cancer."

"Sorry," Billy said. "Looks like you're off the hook, Dan. And I'm glad."

"I can go home now?" Dan asked.

"Yes. If there are any more questions, I know where to find you."

Dan headed for the door. "May I ask a question? Did you drain the fluid from my brakes?"

"No. That was Will Sands. He didn't like you getting ahead of him. But he won't do anything like that again. We had a little talk." Billy smiled at Dan.

"Good. Thanks, Billy. Good night." Dan started to leave.

"One more thing, Dan," Billy said. "There'll be a new foreman here tomorrow. And I think you'll be working quite a few hours now. My work is finished, so I'll be leaving. I'm going to tell the new man that you should be the one to take my place."

Dan grinned. "Tell him I'll be here first thing in the morning." He was whistling as he walked into the cool night.